Loudmouth George and the CORNET

LOUDMOUTH GEORGE and the CORNET

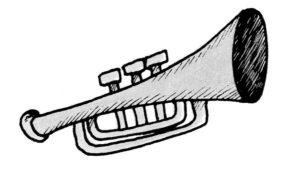

NANCY ★ CARLSON

Carolrhoda Books, Inc. / Minneapolis

For Kathy Mack, who called Carolrhoda for me

First Avenue Editions
An imprint of Lerner Publishing Group
241 First Avenue North
Minneapolis, MN 55401 U.S.A.

Website address: www.carolrhodabooks.com

Library of Congress Cataloging-in-Publication Data

Carlson, Nancy L.
    Loudmouth George and the cornet / Nancy Carlson
        p.   cm.
    Summary: George's cornet playing is too much for both his family and the band.
    ISBN: 1–57505–725–5 (pbk. : alk. paper)
    [1. Rabbits—Fiction. 2. Cornet—Fiction. 3. Bands (Music)—Fiction.
I. Title.
PZ7.C21665bLn 2004
[E]—dc22   2003023706

Manufactured in the United States of America
1 2 3 4 5 6 – JR – 09 08 07 06 05 04

George got a lot of presents for his birthday, but his very favorite came from Uncle Chuck. It was a brand-new, shiny, brass cornet.

"Oh, boy!" said George. "I'm going to be a star!"

George played his cornet every day for a week.

By Saturday he thought he was really good.

"Hey, Mom," he said, "listen to me play 'Moon River.'"

"Pretty good, huh?" said George when he'd finished.

His mom didn't say a word.

I must be even better than I think, thought
George. I left her speechless! It's time I had a
bigger audience.

On Monday, George joined the school band.
"All of our members take lessons after school,"
said Mr. Sharp, the band director. "Let's see, I can
fit you in on Mondays at 4:30."

"That sounds like a lot of work," said George. "Besides, I don't need lessons. I'm already great."

"Well, we'll try you out for a week then," said Mr. Sharp.

On Tuesday, George went to his first rehearsal.
Most of the members were just learning to play their
instruments. George was a little annoyed.

Mr. Sharp had them warm up by playing scales.

Then he directed them on "Three Blind Mice."

"This is pretty boring stuff," said George to Harriet, who sat next to him. "Why don't you come over to my house after school, and I'll teach you how to play 'Moon River.'"

"No thanks," said Harriet.

On Wednesday, Tony was practicing his flute.
"Isn't that beautiful," sighed Harriet.

"I don't think he quite has it," said George.
"Here, Tony, let me show you how it's done."

"That band has a lot to learn," George told his family that evening.

Then he went upstairs to play "Moon River."

On Thursday, Mr. Sharp asked the class if anyone would like to play a solo.

"I would! I would!" said George.

"How about you, Harriet?" said Mr. Sharp.

"That was very good," said Mr. Sharp when
Harriet had finished. "Anyone else?"
"Me! Me! Let me play!" said George.
"How about you, Ralph?" said Mr. Sharp.

"Very nice," said Mr. Sharp when Ralph was through.

"Let me! Let me!" yelled George. "I want to play now."

"Oh, all right, George," said Mr. Sharp.

I'll give them a real treat, thought George.

On Friday, Mr. Sharp asked George to stay after practice.

"George," he said, "I'm afraid I'm going to have to ask you to quit the band."

"Quit!" said George. "But what will you do without me?"

When George got home, he told his mom the news.
"Oh, George," she said, "I'm so sorry."

"Never mind, Mom," said George. "That band was pretty crummy, and I was getting a little tired of playing the cornet anyway. . . ."

"I'm going to take up the tuba instead!"